THE DIRTY DOCTOR'S TOUCH

A BILLIONAIRE DOCTOR ROMANCE

ALIZEH VALENTINE

HOT AND STEAMY ROMANCE

CONTENTS

Blurb   v

1. Chapter 1   1
2. Chapter 2   6
3. Chapter 3   11
4. Chapter 4   16
5. Chapter 5   21
6. Chapter 6   26
7. Chapter 7   31
8. Chapter 8   36
9. Chapter 9   42
10. Chapter 10   46
11. Chapter 11   50
12. Chapter 12   55

Sign Up to Receive Free Books   61
Preview of Whips and Chains   63
Chapter One   65
Chapter Two   69
Chapter Three   73
Chapter Four   79

Other Books By This Author   85
Copyright   87

Made in "The United States" by:

Alizeh Valentine

© Copyright 2020 – Alizeh Valentine

ISBN: 978-1-64808-022-7

ALL RIGHTS RESERVED. No part of this publication may be reproduced or transmitted in any form whatsoever, electronic, or mechanical, including photocopying, recording, or by any informational storage or retrieval system without express written, dated and signed permission from the author

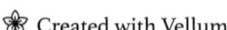 Created with Vellum

BLURB

Dirk

I am a master. An elitist. I am at the top of my field, and I know what I am doing.
Women want me. They worship me. They come to me to fulfill all their needs—all of them.
I can have any one of them I want. But I only want her.
A goddess with a perfect body. So pure, so vulnerable. She takes notice of me, but I obsess over her.
I know how this game is played, and I know she can have her pick of the lot as well. Anyone would be lucky to have her, and everyone knows it.
No matter what, no one else can have her. Everyone wants her, but only I can have her.
I will have her.
I need her.

Charli

I am young, strong and smart. I can make it in this world.
I know I am beautiful, and my beauty is the kind that the world finds captivating. I turn heads everywhere I go. I might not act like I notice, but I do.
Yet, life is a game. Love is a game. Beauty is a game.
I am beautiful, right?
Everyone is telling me to change. I'm not good enough as I am. I need to be better.
I want to be on top of the world, but I feel knocked to my knees. I will rise again.

CHAPTER 1

Charli

"No, no, no! Come on, Baby, focus! Focus!"

I cringe as my Uncle Harvey walks over, his notebook tucked under his arm and a pen behind his ear. With round, mirrored sunglasses that would do John Lennon proud and a bowler cap pulled down to his eyebrows, he doesn't quite pull off the eccentric look—although he certainly is trying. Of course, no one is going to say that out loud. As one of the biggest producers in Hollywood, Harvey Sykes can look however he wants and still have the respect of everyone in the room.

"I'm sorry, can we try it again?" I ask, already knowing what he's going to say.

"We're going to have to. That was deplorable acting. I would have thought that my own flesh and blood would have it a little more together than that!" He shakes his head as he walks away, making gestures to the sound guy and the film guy.

I feel my cheeks flush red. This is the first day going through the scene, and I feel like I am the only one who is causing any kind of issues.

Here I am, trying to live my dream, and I feel like I'm floundering. There are more A-list actors present than I can count, and I can't even remember how to get a single line out of my mouth without screwing it up somehow. My uncle isn't being much help, either. I know that he is the only reason I am standing here today. I am well aware of that.

He's only reminded me thirty times. Today.

I know I shouldn't complain. It's true, he is the only reason that I've made any progress in Hollywood so far. If it weren't for Uncle Harvey, I'd be just like any other young girl from San Francisco with a dream of becoming a star on the big screen—and not having quite as much talent as I'd like to think, to back up those dreams.

"I want to take this scene from the top. Remember, Charli, never look directly into the camera. Look this way—that's right—toward the marker on the wall. We'll do the rest." He's making all kinds of gestures with his hands as he's talking, and I really am doing my best to follow along—though if I'm being completely honest, I'm not quite sure I do understand where he's telling me to look.

Of course, I'm not going to say so. I already feel like everyone else is snickering under their breath at my so-called performance, and the last thing I want to do is make it worse. Uncle Harvey thought he was doing me a favor giving me the lead role in his next big blockbuster film, but so far I feel like I am going to single-handedly tear it apart. I'm trying to get through my lines, but in the back of my mind, I can already see the headlines and the reviews.

Worst movie of the year.

Charli Sykes's career is over before it began.

Thank God for the supporting roles, the lead was a complete joke.

I try not to let my imagination get the better of me. Suddenly, I realize that it's my turn.

"I'm sorry, Jacob, but it's not working anymore. We've tried. Don't ever tell me that I didn't!" I feel proud of myself. I delivered my lines perfectly that time, and I can only imagine the congratulations my uncle is going to give me when we've finished.

"And, scene!" the director shouts.

I walk over to my uncle—no, I strut over to him, feeling more like one of the stars who are drinking mimosas on the sidelines and watching me make a complete fool out of myself.

"What did you think?" I ask coyly. He doesn't even bother to look up at me.

"Awful."

"What!"

"That was atrocious. Charli, who are you talking to? What emotions are you trying to convey? You may as well be breaking up with a jar of mayonnaise as the love of your life. That was simply awful," he shakes his head in disappointment. "And what's this?" He motions to the sweatshirt I'm wearing, and I look down self-consciously.

"It's a hoodie," I lamely remark.

"I can see that, but what in the hell are you doing wearing it here?"

"Jack said that we aren't going to be in costume until later—" I try, but he interrupts.

"I don't give a damn what Jack said. Costume or not, you're going to have to start looking the part if you are going to get into this business." He reaches forward and blatantly unzips the top of my hoodie, revealing far more cleavage than I am comfortable sharing.

"Excuse me! What do you think you're doing?" I snap.

"I'm helping you, and Baby, you need all the help you can get," he replies in an icy tone. "If you are going to be a celebrity, start looking like one."

"I don't have the figure of a celebrity!" I retort, masking the hurt in my voice.

"Not yet, but you will. Look at this and let me know what you think." He hands me a brochure for a plastic surgeon in town, and I laugh.

"What, do you want me to get a nose job?" I sneer.

"Not quite. Open it." I obey, and to my horror, I can see he's underlined the breast augmentation section.

"No!" I say, trying to hand the brochure back to him. He raises his eyebrow.

"What?"

"I'm not getting a boob job!"

"Oh, yes you are."

"Over my dead body."

"Actually, over your dead career." He pulls out the contract I signed a few days before. I have to admit, I didn't read it through as thoroughly as I should have, and my heart sinks. After opening it and flipping through a few pages, he shows me where the surgery was listed as mandatory—and where I signed that I would comply.

"I didn't know that was in there!" I try to argue, but he slips the contract back in the pages of the notebook.

"That's not my problem. If you want to star in this movie, you'll look the part. If you don't, then you'll be in breach of contract and I'll be forced to take legal action against you." He turns to go.

"You mean you'd sue your own niece?" I say, mustering as much attitude as I can. I wouldn't put it past him, but at the same time, I am going to do my best to rub in the guilt while I still can. He's used to this game, and I'm not. He knows what he's doing and he does it well.

"Well, I suppose that wouldn't look good for publicity's sake, but at the same time, neither does breaching your first contract as an actress. If you would agree to ending your acting career and going home, then I would drop the charges. But Charli, don't think you can get the best of me. I have eyes and ears everywhere." He smiles at me and I'm reminded of why my mother always called him the creepy uncle.

But, he has a point. With a sigh, I look through the brochure once more. This is what actors and actresses do. They modify themselves to look the part. I should be glad for the opportunity, he tells me.

With a sigh I finally shove the brochure in the pocket of my hoodie.

"Fine, I'll look into it." I try to be a diva, but he merely smiles.

"Excellent. Hollywood is going to look good on you."

CHAPTER 2

Charli

"All you have to do is walk in there and tell them your name, everything else is taken care of." My uncle's voice sounds more irritated than anything as it comes through my phone.

"I didn't make an appointment, though."

"Angela did it for you, just like I already told you. Your job is to show up and look the part. Agents take care of everything else." He sounds exasperated.

"I guess I'm just not used to that," I say, using my diva voice.

"Welcome to Hollywood, Baby." He hangs up the phone before I have the chance to say anything else, and I shake my head.

I love acting and living in Hollywood, but I can't say that I'm ever going to get used to this lifestyle. At least, I don't think I am. I've always been the one in charge of getting things done in my life, how am I just going to hand that responsibility over to some agent and hope they do it the right way?

Even now, as I take the elevator up to the ninth floor to the plastic surgeon's office, I'm not convinced that the receptionist is going to know who I am when I tell her my name. I walk down the long hall, following the signs on the wall rather than suffering through the embarrassment of asking for directions.

Finally, I find the right place and open the door. There are a few women seated in the waiting room, and one man. The man looks up from his magazine and eyes me as I walk in, but I ignore him. There are more aspiring actors and actresses in this town than I know what to do with. I honestly don't care what movie he's working on, or what kind of plastic surgery he needs to get the part.

I don't even want my imagination to go in that direction.

The receptionist is seated in a room behind sliding glass, and I feel awkward as I look around for a way to get her attention. She's not on the phone, but she's not looking at me, either. Shyly, I lightly tap on the glass and she turns, looking annoyed. After holding up a finger and taking her time finishing whatever it was she was doing, she slides open the glass with a rather loud bang.

"Can I help you?"

"Yes, my name is Charli Sykes, and I'm here for a consultation with Dr. Carr." I try to sound important, but she is already running her finger down a list of names on a sheet of paper. I can't help but wonder why it's not in the computer system, but I don't say anything.

"What's the consultation for?" she asks as she looks up.

"Um, plastic surgery," I say lamely.

"Of course, honey, everyone is in here for plastic surgery. I mean what kind?" She has a very rude tone to her voice, and I want to tell her to back off. But I'm already dying of embarrassment, and I don't want to make this situation any worse.

"Breast augmentation," I say in a low voice.

"Pardon?"

"Breast augmentation!" I say flatly. I can hear the sound of magazine pages rustling behind me, and can only imagine the smirks on their faces. She holds my gaze for a moment, then looks at the list.

"Oh yes, I see you're down for 1:30 PM. You've got ten minutes to wait." She points with her pen to one of the seats, and I hesitate as I look around.

"I was hoping if I arrived early I might get in a little earlier," I say, and she looks at me with a smug look on her face.

"That's not how it works here, sweetie."

I spend the ten minutes waiting with my eyes glued to the front of a cooking magazine. I'm not sure why they have this in a plastic surgery waiting room, but I guess I can't complain. At last, the nurse opens the door and calls my name, and though I refuse to look around, I can feel the stares of everyone in the waiting room.

"I see you are here for a breast augmentation consultation?" The nurse smiles and I feel somewhat more at ease.

"Yes, and I'm really not sure what to expect. Should I put on a gown?"

"No, no, not this time. He's just going to talk to you—let you know what you can expect in the procedure and the process. I'll let him know you're in here." The nurse leaves and I sit on the examination table, hoping to just get this over with.

When the door opens, I expect an old man to walk in. Instead, I look up to find the hottest man I've ever seen in my life.

"Miss Sykes? Hello, Dr. Dirk Carr. How are you?" He extends his hand and I take it, fumbling over my words.

I do my best to focus on what he is saying, but the way he smiles when he looks at me is making it difficult for me to concentrate on anything. Suddenly, I realize he's asked me a question.

"I'm sorry?"

"I asked how old you are. You seem very young, and this is quite a procedure. It's something I want all my clients to be certain of before they do." He smiles and my cheeks burn.

"I'm twenty-three." I say, feeling ashamed that I am trying to sound grown-up. I want to ask him how old he is—he looks way too young to be one of the top surgeons in this town—but he continues.

"May I see?" he asks. My smile fades.

"See?"

"Yes, your breasts. I need to know what we're starting with if I can tell you what we're going to end up with," he laughs. I awkwardly unzip my hoodie and take it off, leaving me sitting there in just my skimpy tank.

"The shirt and bra too, if you don't mind." I feel as though I'm going to pass out. Of course I mind. But I guess this is what I'm here for.

He reassures me and gives me his best doctor speech as I reluctantly pull my top off and unclasp my bra, watching his face as I pull it away. It's nearly impossible to read past the professionally vacant expression in his eyes, though I'm certain he appears to be pleased with what he sees.

"Okay, so it says here that you are hoping to go up at least two cup sizes, perhaps even three—is that correct?" I am sitting with my shirt off and my breasts hanging out. The last thing I want to talk about now is cup sizes. But, I know that he is waiting for an answer, and I nod.

"I guess. That's what my uncle told me I needed for the movie," I say.

He looks up with an amused smile. "Sounds like something he'd want."

I'm surprised. "You know who he is?"

"Harvey Sykes, the producer."

I want to know how he knows that, but he doesn't elaborate. Instead, he has me lie back on the table and lays a towel over me, finally covering my chest. Then he picks up a chart and begins to show me the different kinds of breasts. While I'm trying to focus on what he's saying and answer his questions, I just want to die.

I can't believe this gorgeous man has just seen me without my shirt on.

CHAPTER 3

Dirk

Another aspiring actress in room fourteen.

My receptionist, Angie, has seen so many of these girls walk through my doors that she doesn't bother with professionalism anymore. Not with me anyway. We often trade notes and laugh about how the appointments went afterwards. Though Angie is happily married to another woman, she still appreciates a young woman's body and wants to know every detail I can share after a new client leaves the room.

This is routine for me. Mundanely routine. I'll go in there, I'll tell her that the procedure's going to be really expensive, and she'll tell me she'll get her rich boyfriend to pay for it. Plain and simple.

I'm surprised, however, when I read the name on the chart. Charli Sykes. I've never met the girl in person, but I've seen plenty of photos of her.

Her uncle and I have worked together many times throughout the years. In fact, he's my number one referral. His clients come in all shapes and sizes, from all backgrounds, but they all only want one thing. Part of me wonders why he would send his niece in here—from the photos he's shown me she already looks like she's star material.

Another part of me is glad he did.

I go into the room and I find I'm surprised again. She's much more shy and nervous than my typical client. Usually my patients know exactly what they want and aren't shy about telling me, but there's something different about Charli.

I make small talk with her and I tell her the basics, then it comes time for the big reveal. As much as I try to be professional, a little part of me is excited as I ask her to take off her shirt and bra. Don't get me wrong, it's not her alone that I get this thrill for—I love it any time I have a star actress sitting on my table.

Of course, the more experienced actresses are more than willing to rip their top off for any guy who asks, but there's something so innocent about the newly arrived actresses who have yet to make it big. I don't see as many of the fresh-faced girls as I'd like—when you've made a name for yourself like I have, you get to work with the biggest names in the business—but it's always a treat when one of them is sitting on my table. They're not as jaded—they move slowly, they do their best to cover themselves though it's my job to look at the thing they're trying to hide. They are just so pure and untouched by fame.

For now.

Charli is no different from the rest as far as shyness goes. In fact, she might be even more shy than many of the first timers. It's clear she doesn't want to take her shirt off, and once she has it off, she doesn't want me to look at her breasts.

"Don't worry, I'm a professional, and I'm going to give you my professional opinion," I try to reassure her. But as soon as her shirt comes off, I find it incredibly difficult to be professional. For the first time in my entire career, I want nothing more than to take this young woman right here on my table.

Her breasts are perfect—her body is perfect. They are a little on the small side for Hollywood, but they are perfectly shaped and exquisitely proportioned to the rest of her body. I get to take them in my hands, but I can't fondle them like I'm dying to do.

I want to bury my face in them and breathe her in deeply. I want to lick and suck on her nipples. I want to take her so hard —but I have to hide all of these feelings and maintain a professional atmosphere. It would be a lot easier if I didn't have these beauties right there in front of my face, so, I ask her to lay back and I cover her with a towel—something I never do.

I've never reacted this way with a patient before, and I need to clear my head. I've seen more breasts than I can ever remember, so what's so different about Charli?

I can concentrate a little better with her torso covered, though it's difficult for me to go over the charts with her. Of course, I know how to mask how I'm feeling—I've done it a thousand times with other women before, hiding your thoughts and emotions is simply part of being a doctor—but this is the first time I have ever felt truly challenged in doing this. I can see Charli is doing her best to focus on the charts, but she seems distracted. I can only imagine it's because she's not used to taking off her top for strange men she's just met, and part of me is pleased.

"I just really want it to look—well, natural," she says at last.

I look down at her. Her young, beautiful face looks unsure, and I feel bad for her. Of course she wants to look natural, and I know I could do something for her that she would probably love. But, on the other hand, I'm not so sure that I want to play any part in changing her gorgeous body.

"Real natural beauty is far better than any falsely natural look in my opinion," I hear myself saying. I don't mean it as bluntly as it comes out, and she immediately looks up at me with wide eyes.

"What do you mean?"

"Well, Miss Sykes, if I'm going to be perfectly honest with you—and I am—I don't know why your uncle wants you to get this done. Your body is perfect just as it is." I smile as I speak, and I can see by the look in her eyes she doesn't believe me. However, her face flushes a deep, crimson red and I know I've flattered her.

"He says every woman in Hollywood has breasts like those." She points to one of the models on the chart I was showing her, and I shake my head.

"There are plenty of successful actresses who have smaller breasts. Look, I'm not trying to talk you out of this, I just want you to be sure that it's what you want before you go through with it." I smile and she looks away.

It's clear that she is torn about something, and I would do anything to help her. She suddenly looks up at me.

"If I were to go through with it, what would the cost be to go up two sizes?" I feel my heart sink a bit. I don't know what's wrong with me—here is a client coming from one of the wealthiest producers in Hollywood. I could quote her whatever I liked and he would be more than happy to pay, knowing that I'd produce a work of art that would turn heads everywhere she went from here on out.

But then, I don't really want to do the surgery. I don't want this girl to make herself look fake because her uncle thinks she should. I want to show her what it's like to be appreciated for who she is—just how she is. She's perfect. I reluctantly pick up another book and flip it open, naming her several quotes. I can't help but smile when her eyes widen.

"Your uncle is going to pay for this, I assume?" I ask with a grin. She nods, though she is still white as a sheet.

"Good. Well, think it over and let me know what you decide. Let your uncle know that I cut him a good deal on this, too. I've recently raised my personal fee for such surgeries, and that alone adds several thousand dollars to the cost." I smile once more, and she shakes her head. Suddenly, I realize she is still lying on the table under the towel, and for the first time in as long as I can remember, I feel slightly embarrassed.

"You can get dressed," I tell her—though I would much rather stand there and stare at her perfect body all day.

CHAPTER 4

Charli

I grab my tank and yank it over my head, embarrassed that I'd chosen such a skimpy top to wear. Of course I wore the hoodie over the top, but what must he think of me? Does he think that I normally run about with practically nothing on? Then again, this is Hollywood, and I haven't exactly seen a lot of people concerned about the amount of skin they show in public.

"I hope that I was able to answer all your questions," he says as he watches me put my clothing back on. I refuse to make eye contact with him as I zip up my hoodie once more—zipping it up high enough to hide any cleavage my bra created. There's a part of me that thinks he is almost disappointed that I covered so much of myself, but then, I refuse to let myself think about that.

"Yes, thank you. I think that should be all that he needs to know," I say. I still feel awkward discussing the size of my breasts with anyone, let alone my uncle or this gorgeous man in front of me, but I have no choice.

"Here, let me write a few things down for you that you can

pass along. That way you'll be certain to remember everything." Dr. Carr smiles as he scribbles a few things down on a piece of paper in his notebook. He tears the page free and hands it to me, then he hands me a few more brochures.

"Just so you know for sure what you are going to be facing as far as aftercare goes. I know it can be difficult when you are in the middle of a project, and he might want you to get it done as soon as possible. Although once again I can't help but say I don't think this procedure is necessary for you. You're perfect." Dr. Carr clasps his hands behind his back and I blush despite my biggest efforts not to.

"Thank you," I say again. I don't know what else to say. The most attractive man I have ever seen in my life just told me that I have a perfect body—how would any girl respond to that?

I can't help but be a little confused by his assessment. Why would he tell me something that would lose him money? Was he giving me his professional opinion—it's his job to recognize beauty, after all—or was he being a little more personal?

He opens the door and points me down the hall, and I give him a small wave as I leave.

I can't get him out of my mind the entire drive back to my apartment. I know I have to get down to the studio and meet with my uncle, but I'm going to take a minute to change into something a little less revealing first.

His black hair. His dark blue eyes. I think I might have even detected the bottom part of a tattoo when he rolled up his sleeves to examine me.

To examine me! The memory of that man with my breasts cupped in his hands is almost more than I can bear. I can feel a heat in my loins as I drive and I shake my head.

I've only ever been with one other man in my life—and he could hardly be considered a man. My boyfriend and I had slept together on prom night, and I had to admit, it was a huge letdown. I tried to excuse it as us both being eighteen and not knowing what we were doing, but ever since that night I've never really wanted to have sex with anyone in else. It just didn't seem exciting after my disappointing experience.

I was too busy with my acting career to worry about boys in college, and now here I am, dreaming about the man who has given me a breast exam for surgery. Maybe it's time for me to reassess my celibate lifestyle. I shake my head, clearing my thoughts of the doctor.

I have to find my uncle.

"And this is everything?"

"That's everything he gave me besides this bit of advice. He doesn't think I should go through with the surgery."

"What? Why?" Uncle Harvey looks at me with raised eyebrows. I can't tell if there is concern in his eyes or not, but I continue anyway.

"He says my body is perfect just the way I am. He doesn't think that I need surgery to fix anything." I smirk, but it fades when my uncle bursts into laughter.

"Well, that's why he's in that line of work, and I'm in this one. Excellent. I want you to give them a call and set an appointment right away. During recovery we can film some of the slower scenes. And you can use that time to work on your lines." He beams as he turns on his heel and walks away, but I can't help but call after him.

"I don't think I really need to—"

"Remember the contract!" he shouts back. I sigh. There is no winning.

I wait until the next day to call.

The phone rings and rings, and I can't help but think that the receptionist is sitting there, letting it ring off the hook as she stares blankly at the computer screen in front of her. When the answering machine picks up, I am tempted just to hang up and try again later.

On impulse, I decide to leave a message.

"This is Charli Sykes. I wanted to set an appointment for surgery, so if you could give me a call back as soon as you get this, I would very much appreciate it." I leave my number and hang up, skeptical that the receptionist will ever call me back—she didn't seem to be too fond of me when I was in the office. Now, it's time to focus on the rest of the day.

It's not until late in the afternoon when my phone finally rings. I look down, and not recognizing the number, answer. I'm surprised to hear Dr. Carr's voice on the other end of the line.

"Hey, I got your message and was just giving you a call back," he says.

"I thought that's what you have a receptionist for." Why am I teasing him?

"She's out at lunch, and I didn't want to leave you hanging. Anyway, there are a few more things I would like to discuss with you before we go ahead and set the date for the surgery, but I would prefer to discuss it over lunch rather than in the office." He speaks casually, but my guard is up.

"Lunch?" I ask. It's seems kind of strange for a plastic surgeon to discuss a procedure over lunch, but maybe that's just the way people do things in this town.

"Sure, no doubt you'll want to get away from all the stress of the set for an hour or two. Besides, you're technically going to still be working." He laughs at his little joke and I can't help but smile in spite of myself. It wasn't a date, after all, but I could always pretend.

"How about going down to Starsky's?" he asks and I almost drop my phone. That is a five star restaurant, and one of the most expensive ones in town at that. My lunch alone would cost me a week's salary. I hesitate, not knowing how to answer.

"This is a client lunch, so I'll pick up the tab," he prompts. That is an offer I can't refuse, and though I feel strange doing it, I hear myself accepting his invitation.

"Excellent. Then I will see you tomorrow at one if that works for you?"

"One o'clock works fine for me. See you then, and thank you." I hang up the phone, ignoring the flutter in my stomach. I'll probably never get used to the way they do things around here.

CHAPTER 5

Dirk

I don't make a habit of taking my clients to lunch. It's true that I've had some flings with a couple of knockouts who have walked through the doors of my practice, but I know that those relationships never last long. In fact, I prefer that they don't. And I never start anything until after my work with them is done, never before or during.

I have to admit, I wasn't sure how Miss Sykes was going to react to me asking her out to lunch, but I am thrilled that she agreed. One might argue that Starsky's is a little extravagant, but I want to see what this girl is like when she's relaxed. If I were to bring her back into my office, I know she'd be tense and nervous just like she was a couple of days ago.

By taking her out, she'll have the chance to unwind and relax—and that'll give me the chance to see what she's really like when her uncle isn't forcing her into a situation she doesn't wish to be in. Obviously, I would much rather see her lying naked on my bed than clothed and in a restaurant, but there's no way I'm going to get the former, so I may as well settle for the latter and be happy with what I can get.

I offer to send a cab for her, but she declines, insisting she'll meet me at the restaurant. A part of me worries that she might not show up, but I remind myself that she knows this is Hollywood and we do things differently here.

Though I spend the entire morning fantasizing about her perfect body along with her perfect breasts, I manage to pull it together when I see her step out of a cab outside the restaurant.

I motion to the waitress and tell her to bring Miss Sykes to my table, and I see her visibly relax when she spots me.

"My, my! I can't say that I've ever eaten here before." She laughs nervously as she sits down, and I can see at once that she's more relaxed than she was when we were back in my office. Perhaps this is because she knows that I'm not going to be asking her to remove her shirt. Perhaps it's because she knows she's free to drink as many glasses of wine as she wants if she needs to make herself feel comfortable.

"I'm sure your wife and kids love it when you bring them in here," she says, looking up at me from under lashes.

I smile. I'm not sure if she's being genuine or if she's fishing for information, but I am more than happy to oblige.

"Never been married and don't have kids. Though I have to say that you are going to have something to tell your boyfriend when you get home tonight if you've never been in here before." I use her same technique and she takes the bait.

"I don't have a boyfriend. I was too focused on my career to worry about any kind of relationship, and I'm perfectly happy to keep it that way." There is a silence between us, and she sips on her water. I ordered a martini, but I'm only going to sip on it throughout the meal.

After we order our food and get through some small talk, I

am more than ready to dive into the real reason I asked her to meet me.

"I'm not going to tell you what to do with your own body, but I am going to encourage you to think about this. I have seen many young women come to me over the years asking for something like this, only to realize six months later that they've made the wrong choice. I don't want to see this happen to you." I approach the topic carefully, not wanting to intrude on her affairs. I can see by the look in her eyes that she wants to tell me something, but there's something else that is keeping her from doing so.

I try to prompt it out of her. "Sometimes you have to consider the reasons why you'd want to make a drastic change like this…"

"It's just that my uncle feels that this is going to be my big break in Hollywood. I want this more than anything, and I'm scared that if I lose the part, then I'll never get another chance." She looks down into her drink and I laugh.

"If you think that your uncle is the only producer in Hollywood that would love the chance to use you in a film, you're wrong," I say, but she looks up at me with wide eyes. She leans in closer to me, her tone rather hushed, as though she's concerned that someone might overhear what she's about to say.

"He'll sue me if I break the contract. That's what he said. If I don't go through with this then he said I could forget about acting and get a lawyer. I didn't know this was part of my contract—I guess I just trusted him and didn't read through it very well."

I can't help but feel sorry for her. I've known her uncle a long time, and though I'd known he'd done things like this to others, it surprises me that he would do it to his own niece.

Though it goes against my better judgment, I know I have to help her. I can't let her permanently change her body for something like this. If she wanted this, that would be one thing, but since she's clearly unwilling, it is quite another. I don't want to be complicit in what her uncle is pulling on her. I lean in as well.

"Let me tell you something, your uncle's bark is a lot worse than his bite. I know you don't have the money to take on someone like him, but if you decide that you don't want to go through with the surgery and he tries anything stupid, then you let me know and I'll hire the best lawyer in the country to defend you." I smile warmly down at her, and she looks at me with grateful eyes. I can clearly see she isn't sure how to respond, though I finally see some of the worry leave her eyes.

I try to loosen things up further. "So, you're an actress?"

Her face brightens. "Yes! This is my first role, and my uncle says that I'm a natural. Listen to this 'how do you know he's not going to fall in love with me at the touch of my sultry lips on his own?'"

She seems immediately embarrassed at her recitation, but I clap.

"Very good! I have to say, he's right. That was pure talent right there."

Though she's still clearly embarrassed by what she just did, Charli also tries to make this situation more natural by asking me how I got into plastic surgery.

"I've always enjoyed taking something beautiful and making it all the more so. It's art, like what you do, just a little different." I can see that my words have an effect on her, and she doesn't fully know how to respond. She seems a lot more intrigued by me now, and I'm dying to see more of her acting.

"Here, let me give you my personal number. You can still get a hold of me at the office at any time, but I want to make sure you have a way to get a hold of me for any reason." I jot down my number on a napkin and hand it to her, and I am pleased as she puts it in her purse.

"Thank you so much, I don't know what I would do if he came after me," she says quietly. On another impulse, I reach across the table and put my hand over hers. I feel a shock run through me as our hands touch, but I merely smile.

"You've got a friend in me, I promise," I say warmly. Now that some of the burden of her decision has been lifted from her shoulders, I can see her melting in my hands. I have no doubt I could very easily make her mine.

CHAPTER 6

Charli

"Clearly the man is into you! Come on, spill the beans—how old is he?" I can't help but smile. I didn't know if I should tell anyone about my lunch with the doctor, but I couldn't keep it a secret from my best friend Maddison. Now she's all over the idea, wanting to know every single detail.

"He's thirty-seven, I looked it up online. Don't you think that's a little old for me?"

"Not at all! Dude! That's great. I'd be fucking his brains out if I were you." I shake my head. Maddison has always been rather adventurous, and I can imagine she means every word she says.

"I don't know. I think he's just being professional. You know—he is a doctor and I'm the client. He has to make sure that I'm taken care of."

"By offering you a lawyer?" she asks incredulously, but I brush off the question. We talk for a while longer before I tell her I have to go and hang up the phone.

Ever since our lunch the day before, I haven't been able to

get the man off my mind. He's all I've been able to think about—what I want to do to him. What I want him to do to me.

I've never been the kind of woman to obsess over sex, even before my one disastrous experience with the act, so why do I want this man inside me so badly? I can't figure it out, but I know it's what I want.

I slip into a nice, steamy shower and let my thoughts drift to the doctor as I run my hands all over my body. I think back to him with his hands around my breasts, and I imagine what could've happened had I been far more sensual than I know I was. By the time I get out of the shower, I am very aroused.

I walk over to the mirror and wipe away the fog to look at myself. I've always seen the flaws in my body, so it really didn't surprise me that much when my uncle brought up the idea of a little enhancement—but that doesn't mean that this hasn't taken a toll on me. I close my eyes as I remember how I felt when the doctor—Dirk, I can't help but think of him by his name—told me that I am perfect just the way I am.

Suddenly, I have an idea. I don't know why, but I grab my phone. He said I could call if I needed to. I don't really have a question—perhaps I'll call it a concern.

Do you think my breasts are shaped right to have this done? I write out in a text. It's the one thing I haven't asked him about—my shape—and though I know that they are fine, I need an excuse to talk to him. I barely have time to wrap a towel around my body when my phone chimes with an answer.

What do you mean?" I smile at the reply.

I don't know if they're – you know – maybe I should get a second opinion? Though I know it's not the best idea, I attach a winking emoji to the end of the text. Flirting with a doctor might be wrong, but it sure is fun.

This kind of concern sounds urgent, I would rather take a look at them again myself before I am able to answer. Why don't you come over?

I smile at the text and feel myself blush, doing my best to think clearly. Of course I want to go over to his house more than anything. I may not have a ton of experience with men, but I know he has to have more in mind than just examining my breasts. It's certainly after what could be considered office hours, so I know he's asking me to go over to his personal apartment.

This is definitely far outside of the realm of what could be considered appropriate doctor-patient behavior, but I can't help it. I have to know more about him. I can't pass up on this opportunity—besides, this is Hollywood, anything can happen here.

I ask him for his address, and within minutes I have a cab on the way. I don't care if this is a good idea or not—I am going to go see the doctor.

I arrive at his apartment with low expectations. I know the man has to have a lot of money, but seeing where he lives blows my mind. I look up, craning my neck to see the top floor. He's leaning against the balcony and motions for me to come inside. In another moment I'm outside his door.

When I walk inside, I am amazed at how the penthouse is decorated. It looks like something out of a movie. Exotic décor, sparkling appliances, beautiful hardwood floors, pricey counter tops, and a rug to die for.

"Please, come in. I've poured you some wine," he says. I follow him inside, but it isn't long before we are out on the balcony. It's a warm night, and the sunset is beautiful. We make as much small talk as I can muster, though we both know why I am here.

"You have a beautiful apartment," I say lamely. He laughs as he hands me my wine.

"I'm glad you think so. I haven't seen yours, but I imagine it must be similar." I laugh.

"Far from it! I can barely afford to get around this town, and I definitely can't afford a place like this." I put my hand on the balcony railing as I look out, and I feel him standing close behind me.

"You could if you found the right connections," he breathes. I can feel his hot breath on my ear, and my loins grow just as hot. I turn slightly, but say nothing. We both hesitate for a moment, and then he leans forward slowly, pressing his lips to mine.

I feel like I've been waiting for this moment forever, and begin kissing him back with as much passion as I have been holding back since meeting him. He deepens the kiss as he wraps his arm around my waist and guides me back in the living room. Without breaking away from him, I set my wine down on the table and put my hands around his face, his neck.

He bends forward slightly and I jump up, wrapping my arms and legs around him. His t-shirt has started riding up his stomach, and I run my hands under the soft material, feeling his strong, chiseled chest. He walks into his bedroom and lays me gently down on the bed. He grabs the hem of my shirt and yanks it up, revealing the lace bra I wore specifically for him. With my shirt off, he begins kissing my neck, working his way down between my breasts, and over my panting, flat stomach.

I have my hands on the buckle of my jeans, and in an instant they're off, revealing matching panties to my bra. He takes a step back and just looks at me, admiring me like no man has before. I am breathing hard, eager to have him. I don't know what's come over me, but I need to have him inside me.

I sit up on my knees on the bed and begin kissing his neck as I lift up his shirt and take it off him completely. He unbuttons his pants but I swat his hands away, continuing with my task of undressing him. A part of me is shocked at how bold I'm being, but I just can't wait a second longer to see his perfect body.

I take him in my mouth briefly, feeling his member pulse

and twitch. He doesn't allow me to stay in control for long, rolling me back on the bed as his hands and mouth go to work exploring every inch of me. He unclasps my bra and it falls away, revealing my stiff nipples.

I don't feel ashamed of my body—I want nothing more than for him to consume every part of me. He pulls my panties down and climbs over me, staring at my wet folds as he fists his beautiful cock and places it at my entrance. I gasp as he thrusts his throbbing self inside of me. He pumps slowly at first, but I can't control the moans that are escaping from my lips as I feel him stretching me.

The more I moan and run my fingers down his back, the harder he pumps himself into me. Never have I experienced sex like this, and I feel like my entire body is going to be torn apart.

Wave after wave of pleasure washes over me, and I can see in his face that he is enjoying himself as much as I am. Then, all at once he gives a final push, and I feel an explosion inside me that tips me over the edge and fills me with more warmth than I ever thought possible. I can feel his member pulse inside me, and I feel like I'm in heaven.

He is breathing just as heavily as I am, and for a moment, our eyes lock.

I feel no shame.

CHAPTER 7

Charli

I open my eyes to sunlight coming in through the slits in the drapes, and I can't help but squint. I don't remember there being such nice drapes over the windows, but I'm impressed when I do see them. I stretch and look around, also surprised to find that I am alone in bed. There is a dent in the pillow where Dirk was sleeping the night before, but besides that, there is no indication that anyone else was ever in the apartment with me.

I get out of bed with a blush flushing my cheeks, grabbing my bra and panties and quickly pulling them on. My jeans are on the floor in a pile next to my shirt, and I am quick to pull those on as well. Though I was feeling bold and proud of myself last night, I can feel a sense of shame rising in my chest. I can't believe I had sex with this man within days of knowing him, and I can't block out the fear of what Dirk is going to think of me—what he must think of me already after last night.

I can't help but wonder if he does this kind of thing with many women—does he think that I'm just some loose woman who's trying to sleep my way to the top? Or am I just another girl in a long list of flings? I tell myself I have no control over it now, though I can't fight the feeling in the back of my mind that I've made a mistake. I tell myself to stop. That is not the way I want to think about last night. That's not the memory I want to have.

Just take a deep breath and get ready to face today, I tell myself. That's all I can do. The more I wake up, the more I realize there is a delightful aroma of coffee wafting into the room from the kitchen. Curious whether the doctor is out there—*Dirk*, I need to start thinking of him by his name—I wander in that direction.

There's hot coffee in the pot next to the stove and a note telling me to help myself. There's no mention of the night before or what I should to do before I leave, so I pour myself a small cup of the hot liquid and look about the apartment. It's a lot different during the light of day, though I have to admit it's every bit as impressive as the night before.

My glass of wine has been poured out and the glass cleaned, and it is now hanging to dry on a rack near the sink. I can't help but smile seeing his glass next to mine, and thinking of him washing them both this morning as he got ready to head to the office. I refuse to allow myself to think of what it would be like if this was how I started my day every morning.

After all, we come from two different worlds.

Suddenly remembering the world I come from, I check the time and I run over to my purse. I pull out my phone to find several text messages and missed calls from my uncle, all saying the same thing—he isn't happy, and he wants me down at the studio as soon as possible. I drain the rest of my coffee and grab my jacket, slipping it on as I head out the door.

"Where have you been? Do you think this is a game? I told you we might need you on set today, and Babe, you haven't played long enough to be able to just go missing like that!" Uncle Harvey says when I step out of the cab. He's waiting for me outside, eager to hear whatever explanation I have to offer.

But I haven't got one.

I don't want to tell my uncle where I was the night before, nor do I want to tell him what I think of the way he has been treating me—I wasn't even supposed to be on set today and he's acting as if I've missed a week of shooting. But I just want him to stop asking questions.

"I'm here now, that's all that really matters." I mutter as I walk past him and toward the building.

"I don't know what's gotten into you, Charli, but let me tell you—I can end this contract just as fast as I started it, and I have a whole line of other women who would be more than happy with the part. You had better shape up or you're done." I keep walking, though my heart is pounding in my chest. I know he's right, and I have to be careful, but I'm going to pretend like I don't care.

The morning goes smoothly but the afternoon drags by slowly. I check my phone several times. The only person who I'd told about the night before was Maddison, and she is more than ecstatic about what she calls my *progress*. I don't know if I would use the same word myself, but if that is what she wants to call it, that's fine with me.

Maddison isn't the reason I keep checking my phone, however. I haven't heard a single word from Dirk. I don't know what I thought I was going to hear, but I had thought he might say something. Anything. We never officially got around to talking about what I was concerned about the night before—we didn't do much talking at all, now that I think back—so it seems he could at least ask me about that, in a more professional capacity. Or it would been nice if he'd ask me if I got out of the apartment alright—it'd just be nice to hear from him at all, before I really start to regret what happened.

When my phone finally does go off and I see it's the doctor, I nearly drop it in the middle of the street. My fingers shake as I unlock it and quickly skim over the words, eager to hear what it is he has to say to me. At this point I'm sure it's going to be something about the upcoming procedure, but I'm thrilled to see it's not.

I had a really good time last night. I'm so glad you were able to stop by. I want you to know that you are simply amazing—absolutely beautiful, just the way you are. You don't need a surgery to fix any of that, and I mean it.

The biggest smile splits my face, and I wait eagerly as I see he's typing another message.

By the way, I am going out with some friends tonight, and I was wondering if you might want to join us? It's been a while since I've had a date and they're beginning to talk. Of course, there's no pressure, but if you think that you might want to have a good time let me know.

I read through the text several times, my heart racing in my chest each time. Is he really asking me to go out with his friends? What are the things these kinds of people like to do? It's clear he isn't hurting for money, and I have to assume he hangs out with other people from his pay grade. In other words, people who probably hang out places that are way out of my league. On the other hand, if I were to go as his guest, then he'd probably be paying for me. Well, that's one less thing to worry about.

I get in the cab once shooting is over and set my phone down on the seat, thinking. My uncle is still furious with me over this morning, but I don't really care. I am glad last night happened, and the brief feeling of shame that I had this morning has faded into nothing. Now, I want to see more of this life that feels so forbidden. I want to go out with a handsome, successful man and learn the kinds of things these people do when they go out.

Now is my chance to get a glimpse at the lavish Hollywood lifestyle I've always dreamed of, to be a part of that group.

And if the only thing that happens tonight is that I get to spend an evening on Dirk's arm, well that'll be worth it on its own.

Silently, I promise myself I'm going to be responsible, and I'll make sure I get home at a decent hour. I'll only have a couple of drinks before I switch to water, and I'll be up bright and early in the morning and ready to go on set.

Tomorrow, this will just be a memory, but it's going to be one that I'll be glad to have.

CHAPTER 8

Dirk

I don't know what it is about this girl, but I can't get her off my mind. Driving to work, she was the only thing I wanted to think about. At work, I can hardly concentrate on the other women who are coming through the doors. Each of them expects top of the line treatment—and that means giving them my undivided attention—but the only woman whose body I want to think about is Charli.

I don't want to seem desperate—a feeling I haven't had in as long as I can remember. At the same time, I don't want her to feel as though our night together was just a fling and that I don't care about her. Part of me expects to receive a text from her, but common sense is telling me that I'm not going to. Of course she's going to wait for me to text her first.

She probably wants to know what page I'm on before she puts herself out there any more than she did last night.

"Hey, Dirk. We're going out later with some of the guys, you want to come?" Rob, another surgeon at my practice, peeks his head into my office to ask.

I haven't been out with the group for a while, and know that I owe it to them to have some fun. But I don't want to do anything other than see Charli again. Suddenly, I have an idea.

"There's a new girl in town that could use a few introductions, mind if I bring her along?"

"Bring whoever you want."

It would be a great way for her to see what it's like living the celebrity life in Hollywood, and it would be a great way for me to spend more time with her. I want her to see that she can make connections and get out there and be herself without having to alter her body—even though I hardly know her, I'm confident she'll fit right in with my scene. She just has some quality to her that I know will draw people like a moth to a flame, and I don't know why, but I really don't want her to go through with the surgery. Why mess with something that's already so perfect?

I shoot her a text early on in the afternoon. I want to catch her before she has the chance to make plans with anyone else, but I still want to play it safe. I don't want to come on too strong and scare her off. I get the impression she really likes me, but it's difficult to know exactly where to set the boundaries with her. Getting involved with a prospective patient like this is tricky, and I'm sure she's even more confused than I am with this new terrain.

I can hardly believe it when she accepts my invite, though I have to say that I am incredibly relieved. I tell her to put on her best dress and be ready for me to pick her up at seven.

Tonight is going to be the night of her life. I'm going to make sure of it.

I SHAKE my head when she walks down the stairs and gets into the cab.

"Is that what you're wearing?" I ask. She looks down at her knee length skirt and blouse.

"Yes?"

"That will never do." I tell her bluntly, and see her face fall. Shit. "You look cute in that, but if you're going to act like us, you're going to have to look like us," I clarify, happy to see her spirits lift again. "Come on, I'm going to take you somewhere you can get any dress you like—as long as I approve." I wink at her flirtatiously, and though she looks a little doubtful, she doesn't argue.

I tell the cab driver to take us downtown, and I'm surprised at how quickly we are able to find something. Something skimpy.

She looks amazing in everything she tries—it still blows my mind that anyone would think she should change her body—but it only takes a couple of outfits before we find the one. She looks good.

We head to one of the local hot spots and I introduce her to my friends and colleagues. Throughout the evening I can't keep my eyes off her. It seems to me that everyone is as charmed by her as I am, though she keeps looking back at me with wide eyes every now and then.

It's evident that she has never experienced so much luxury at one time, between the bar and the people she's being introduced to, and I'm pleased to say that I am the one who has shown all of it to her. There is something about her that mesmerizes me, and I do feel as though she is mesmerized by the evening itself.

I find her staring at me more than once, and though most of the looks we share send chill shivers of excitement down my spine, there are a couple of times where I believe she is almost jealous. Perhaps it was the way I was looking at that waitress? We are in the most expensive restaurant in town, of course she's going to see a lot of wealthy and well-endowed women. That's the name of the game here, and if she wants to keep up, she's going to have to get used to these sights.

"Are you alright?" I ask as I take a seat next to her. She gives me a cold glance.

"Why do you ask?"

"I couldn't help but notice the way you were watching me just now," I say. She gives me a snapping look, and I lean back in my chair. I don't want to have any problems with her, but I can sense when there is an issue with a woman.

"I couldn't help but notice the way you were watching her," she says with a glance toward our waitress. I laugh.

"Are you jealous? Honey, that's the way Hollywood is. We flirt and we have fun. Get out there and do it yourself!" I try to encourage her to do the same, but she won't budge.

It's clear how much she likes me, and I can't help but love her for it.

"Are you guys coming or what?" Jasmine, one of my colleague's girlfriend, pokes her head around the bar. I am about to reply when Charli speaks up.

"Sure am!" She is up in a flash and the two of them are on the dance floor. The way she looks at me tells me she is trying to get my attention, and it's working. I can't stand it after a few minutes, and I begin raunchily dancing with another woman. It's not long before Charli has made her way over to me and cuts in, dancing right in front of me.

I put my hands on her hips and we move together – I can see she is having just as much fun as I am. Her confidence shines through, and I can't help but want her even more than I did before.

But, as the evening continues, I find that I can't keep my eyes off of her either. More than once I feel that twinge of jealousy as I see the way she looks at some young man closer to her age. I know I'm a bit older, but I'm also the one who has caught her eye, and I intend to keep it.

At last, my friends have worn each other out and everyone is ready to go home. I hail a cab for the two of us and help her get seated inside.

"I'll have him drop us off at my place, then I'll drive you over to yours myself," I say with a smile and she nods. She looks tired but happy, and I'm glad that she accepted my invitation this evening.

However, when we get to my place, we don't head over to my car. Instead, we head inside.

The entire ride up the elevator I can't keep my hands off her. I want to touch her—to feel her—to be inside her. The way she's rubbing her hands up my back and in my hair shows me that she feels the exact same way.

By the time we make it inside my door, we're already tearing the clothing off each other. I can't wait. I can't even make it to the bedroom before I'm on top of her, exploring her with my hands and touching every part of her.

I pull her dress off, revealing her beautiful body beneath. She isn't wearing a bra, and I immediately press my hands, then my face to her breasts. I take a deep breath in, inhaling her rich scent. She moans and leans her head back, wrapping her hands around the back of my head as she looks down and smiles at me.

Looking into her beautiful eyes, I feel my heart race faster.

Her hands are all over me, opening the front of my shirt and running all over my chest. She marvels at my tattoos once again but doesn't spend much time on them before she's pulling at my pants, opening the front of them and pushing them down. I moan and shudder, eager to fill her up. I am already hard, and as I run my hand into her panties, I can feel that she is wet and ready for me. I lay her on the couch and pull them down, and before she even has time to think, I am inside her.

She begins moaning and writhing beneath me, and I can hardly contain myself. Every noise she makes drives me closer to the edge, but above all I want to make sure she is satisfied. Her moans grow in intensity, and I begin to thrust harder into her. The more she moans, the harder I want to go, but I can feel that I'm not going to last much longer myself.

As she begins to scream my name, I arch into her and allow myself to cum with her. Hard. We are both panting and looking into each other's eyes, and I feel all the strength rush out of my body. Sitting down on the couch next to her, I reach over and place my hand over hers.

She looks over at me, and our eyes meet. I pull her into my arms and we lay down, snuggling close, but neither of us says a thing.

There really isn't anything to say.

CHAPTER 9

Dirk

The next morning I wake with Charli lying on my chest. I vaguely remember going to bed with her, but I don't remember much after that. After the mind-blowing sex and with the drinks wearing off, all either of us wanted to do was fall asleep. I offered her one of my t-shirts to sleep in if she wanted, but I have to admit, I was glad when she turned me down. Especially when that meant I got to wake up with her naked in my arms.

I lean forward and give her a light kiss on the forehead. She stirs, but doesn't wake, and I gently slip out of bed. I have to shower and get ready to go to work, although it's the last thing I really want to be doing with my day.

All the way to the office I daydream of Charli—for the second morning in a row. No one has ever made me feel the way she does, and I can't get enough of her. I have already left a message on her phone, telling her again how wonderful I think she is and how much I enjoyed our nights together. I know I have to be careful—we aren't dating, and our relationship has largely revolved around the fact that she's trying to decide if she wants me to work on her breasts or not—but I just can't help it.

My day is much like any other day. The clients come drifting in and out of the office, each one wanting some magic cure to fix their body and therefore fix their life—and I no longer feel that I can offer it to any of them. There was a time—not too long ago—when I loved all the new clients coming in. I felt on top of the world each time I got to work on a client and tell them how to fix their problems—and I really did feel like I was helping them fix their lives.

I've been responsible for tummy tucks and face lifts, botox and countless other procedures that men and women were willing to spend hundreds of thousands of dollars for. And more often than not, I would find someone to sleep with for a few months while it suited both our needs. But that isn't how it is with Charli.

With Charli, I see a future. I don't know how and I certainly don't know why, but I see one. I can imagine going home to her every night. I imagine seeing her name in headlines all over the world with the debut of some new film she's starred in. Most importantly of all, I see us.

"There's someone waiting for you in room twelve." Angie says as she passes me in the hall, interrupting my daydream. In the back of my mind, I hope it's Charli, though I know it's not going to be her. I open the door and am immediately surprised to find Carissa Small—a young woman I'd done some work for and ended up having a fling with a few years prior.

Our relationship hadn't lasted more than a few weeks, but it was enough for us both to look back on with fondness. Now, seeing her sitting in my office made my stomach lurch.

"Carissa, how good to see you," I said. It was good to see her, but I didn't want to encourage her in any way. "What can I do for you?"

She described to me what she wanted, and it was nothing more than a routine procedure. Which would've been fine, if she'd ended it at that.

"I was thinking, if you aren't doing anything later, I might stop by and see you," she says. I shake my head.

"Funny you should ask, but I'm afraid that I'm not available right now. I'm sorry." I don't know what to say, and I can see by the look in her eyes that she's far from satisfied by my answer. However, she forces a smile.

"If you say so," she says. I finish with the appointment and rush her out of the office, being as polite as I can without giving her any indication that I want to see her again. She hesitates at the door, but finally leaves, and I breathe a sigh of relief. I fight the urge to text Charli. She isn't my girlfriend, though I wish she was.

I would just have to deal with this on my own.

THERE'S a knock at my door later that night and I get up. I'm not expecting anything, but I can't deny the twinge of hope that it's Charli. I open the door, and it's not.

"Carissa—what are you doing here?" I ask. I don't want to be rude—she is still a client, after all—and allow her to pass by me as she pushes her way through the door and into my apartment.

"I didn't think you quite got the message earlier," she says with a coy smile.

"I understood what you were saying, but like I said, I'm not interested." I smile, but I can see she doesn't believe me. She begins to take off her jacket, and I can see that she's not wearing much, if anything, underneath.

"Carissa, please. I know what we had was fun, but it's over now. It's been over for a while." She tries to kiss me, but I gently take her hands down from my face. I don't want to cause any problems with her, but she isn't taking the hint.

"Come on, baby, come on." She's still trying to kiss me, and I see I'm going to have to get bolder if I'm going to get my point across.

"Carissa, I need you to leave. I'm sorry, but I do." I ignore the hurt look in her eyes. The hurt is short-lived, however, as she grabs her jacket and yanks it over her shoulder, loudly protesting as she heads for the door. She doesn't care who hears her, and at this point, I just want her gone.

She steps into the hallway, and I'm about to sigh in relief and pour myself a drink when I hear chaos break out. Running over to the door, I see Carissa and Charli arguing. Carissa turns to me.

"I see some things will never change." She laughs as she continues up the hall and Charli looks at me—but the hurt in Charli's eyes feel like a dagger in my soul.

"Charli, this isn't what it looks like—nothing happened!" I say loudly. She turns to go, not at all caring what I have to say. "Charli!"

"You heard what she said. Some things never change!" Charli snaps back. I look at her with a defeated look on my face. For the first time in my life, I feel that I have no control with women, and I would do anything to change what just happened.

"Just give me the chance to explain!" I shout as I hear the door of the elevator open. I know she isn't going to stop, but I hope. I close my door with more force than I intend, but I don't care. She didn't give me the chance to explain, and even when I try to call her she's not ready to listen. Directly to voicemail.

With a sigh of frustration, I throw my phone across the room, not caring that it hits the wall hard. I can get a new phone. Phones are easily replaced.

I can't replace Charli.

CHAPTER 10

Charli

I wake up feeling like I was hit by a bus. I did drink more than I should have when I got home last night, but I feel like an idiot. How could I have fallen for some stupid rich doctor's trick? Of course I was going to let him get the best of me—he had everything I thought I ever wanted. No, I wasn't after him for his money, but he represented the wild, carefree lifestyle that I could have fallen in love with.

I could have fallen in love with him. I had fallen in love with him. But clearly I wasn't anything more to him than another fling. And he broke me.

As I look out the window of my little apartment, I hear my phone chime again. I had turned it to silent for most of the night, not wanting to talk to Dirk. Now that the sound is back on, I can hear him trying to get a hold of me. I feel too stupid to even tell him to leave me alone.

I can't believe I let myself fall for his game. Part of me feels guilty that I didn't let him explain himself last night, but I also feel justified. I caught him red-handed—what was there to explain? I didn't need to hear how that wasn't what it looked like, or that he didn't really do anything with the girl who was leaving his room with nothing on but a jacket.

I deserve someone who is going to be honest with me, and that clearly isn't going to be any of these Hollywood rich men who simply want some attractive woman hanging off their arm. I tried to be real with someone, and look where that got me. I'm done with the same old games with different faces. I'm going to play my own game, and I'm going to win.

And that's going to start with a boob job.

I don't care who does it, as long as it's not Dirk Carr. He had his chance to do the surgery, and instead he spent all his time trying to talk me out of it. I was stupid enough to believe him, and I wasn't going to do that again.

I sigh as I toss my phone over onto my pillow and hoist myself up into a seated position. My head is pounding from the wine I drank, but I'm going to have to shake it off and get myself together.

We are going to start with some of the real filming today, and my uncle made sure that I know that I have to be in perfect shape to get started. Right now, I can't imagine doing any kind of love scene or breakup scene with anyone. Just thinking about having to act out anything close to romance makes me think of Dirk, and I feel a fresh wave of pain each time.

I walk into the bathroom, ignoring the swirling questions that are overtaking my mind. It doesn't matter who that girl is, and it doesn't matter what he did with her. It doesn't matter what I feel about him—he never once told me that he loved me or that we had any kind of a future together. He never even asked me to be his girlfriend! In fact, the more I think about it, the more I realize how stupid I was from the beginning.

I saw how he stared at that waitress's boobs when we were out a couple of nights before. I saw how his eyes lingered on another woman's ass as she walked past. It seemed no matter where he looked, there were more women he let his eyes travel over, linger on, and lust about.

I shake my head with a sad smile. I'm brushing my teeth, but my heart isn't in anything I do. All I can think about is the way he looked at me—the way he smelled when we made love. The way he smiled at me when we were together—he really made me feel like I was something special to him. Then, the memory of seeing that woman walking out of his apartment comes rushing back, and I feel the pain rip through my heart once more.

I spit the toothpaste into the sink and rinse my mouth. This isn't a breakup. We weren't together, so this isn't a breakup.

If I keep telling myself that, I know I'll be okay.

IT'S BEEN three months since I have last heard from Dr. Carr. I still haven't gone through with the surgery and I don't know why. I made several appointments and had several consultations, but no one seemed to be good enough for me to trust them with such a permanent procedure. I need to find someone I can trust more than Dirk—someone better—but that seems to be impossible.

He tried for a while to get a hold of me, but I ignored all his calls and texts. My feelings about what happened were too confusing, and I knew I had to devote all my attention to the movie if I wanted to have any chance of making it in this town.

We still haven't started actually shooting the movie yet. We were set to start several times, but nothing ever came of it. There was always someone who wasn't performing up to the standard, and Uncle Harvey wouldn't have it. Of course, now he's harassing me and telling me that I need to get on with this boob job so we can begin shooting, but I feel I can keep him satisfied enough to stop pressuring me if I tell him that I've found someone.

He doesn't care who does it—he was smart enough not to ask me why I decided against Dr. Carr. Perhaps I don't give him enough credit—after all, the two have known each other for years—at least that's what he tells me. If that's true, then he probably knows that I got a little more involved with the doctor than I should have. Seems that's Dr. Carr's habit.

Of course, I can't say that I regret everything. The fling we had was one of the best times of my life, no matter how brief, and I am thrilled to be able to say that I have had some wild experiences with a handsome, experienced man. I hope the pain will subside soon—even though our time together was short and it's been a few months since we've spoken, the way it ended really hurt me. It still hurts.

My father always told me that I was a fighter, and I know I'm going to get through this. Hollywood is full of men—men who aren't going to do that to me. All I really have to do is get this surgery, make my movie, and choose any one I want. Then I'll get back that feeling I had when I was with Dirk. I mean, I know I am being rather optimistic about the kind of man that I'm going to snag next, but a girl can have her dreams.

My phone chimes, and I don't even glance down at it. I know that it's not anyone I wish to speak with, at least, no one that I feel pressured to speak with right now.

It's probably my uncle, but I honestly feel he can wait.

I'm the star of the show, not him.

CHAPTER 11

Dirk

I stare down into the drink in my hand, doing my best to focus on the brown liquid swirling around in the cup with the ice cubes, rather than the thoughts that are running through my brain yet again. I have to be honest with myself—my life is a complete joke. At least, it has been for the past few months. Ever since the night Charli walked out of my apartment and out of my life, everything has lost meaning for me.

I've done my best to throw myself entirely into my practice, but it doesn't seem to matter how hard I try, I can't seem to get back into it like I once was. There was a time when I really believed I was helping people when they came to me. Now, I don't. Every patient reminds me of Charli and how unsure she was, how she was being forced to consider something she didn't want to do—and didn't really need. She was so perfect in every way—from the shape of her neck to the shape of her breasts, down to the curve in her waist and her long legs.

The way she would writhe and move with me when we were

having sex. The way she would look at me with silent admiration when we were out about town. The way she looked the night I took her to get that dress—and saw her in so many different styles that made me want to take her right there in the middle of the store. Who has the right to say she's anything less than perfect? Who has the right to think they can make her better with silicon and plastic?

For the first few days after she left, I was constantly checking my phone. I wanted to tell her that it was all a mistake. I wanted to let her know that I hadn't done anything with Carissa, but she wouldn't listen. The desperation to let her know the truth had briefly become an obsession, before I finally realized it was all pointless.

Now, staring down at the drink in my hand, I can see how she must feel. No doubt she was devastated to see that girl walking out of my apartment. For all Charli knew, she and I were supposed to be together. If she had thought that it was just fun, she wouldn't have been so devastated when she saw Carissa. No, it wasn't just fun for her, and it wasn't just fun for me. And now, my life is miserable.

I have been doing my best at work to stay focused and deliver the same work that I was before, but I've refused to take on new clients. Each woman that comes in asking for the transformation that will change her life looks like a lost cause compared to Charli, and it takes all the patience and self-control I can muster not to tell her so right then and there.

I want to be successful. I want to have the same clientele that I had before, but I know I'm losing them, slowly but surely. I'm losing them.

"Heya Dirk," a voice behind me says. I look over my shoulder, not wanting to talk to anyone, but knowing being rude wasn't going to get me anywhere in this establishment. Dr.

Goodwin, one of the other plastic surgeons in town, sits down on the chair next to me and orders his own whiskey coke. I smile, though my heart isn't in it.

"I heard you lost one of your up-and-coming clients," he says. I wonder how he knows. It was true, the agency that represents Charli called me shortly after that night and told me they would no longer need my services. But, I didn't know it was common knowledge.

"Is that so? Clients come and go all the time, no doubt you've experienced that too."

It was true, though I knew it wasn't what he was talking about.

"Yeah, but this one was special. Harvey Sykes of Sykes' Productions has a niece, and that niece is going to need a little work before she is ready to stand in the spotlight. Of course, you ought to know this—I've heard a rumor she came to you first. Perhaps it was your portfolio? I don't know. You can't win them all." He slaps me on the shoulder a little too hard, and I smile though I want to hit him.

"Every client has the right to choose their own doctor. I just hope she made the right decision," I say with a smile. It's difficult to have this conversation with anyone, let alone the doctor I hate the most. He is clearly oblivious to anything that happened between Charli and myself, which I am happy for. However, I don't know how much more of his banter I can take. Like it or not, he's right—he landed the client, he's the winner, and I am the one losing the woman of my dreams.

"Just make sure you don't screw it up," I say as I rise from my seat.

"You aren't done, are you? Come on, have another, on me!" He laughs as he slaps the seat where I was just sitting, and I hold up my hand and shake my head. I don't want to argue with him, but I'm certainly not going to sit here and listen to him gloat.

"I've really got to be getting back to some things," I lie. He eventually gives up and I leave, more than ready to get away from there. I don't usually mind the friendly banter between my rivals, but I can't stand hearing that he is going to be putting his hands on Charli—he's going to ruin her perfect form and leave on it his own mark. He's going to destroy everything I tried so hard to build up in that girl.

I hail a cab and get inside, shoving my hands in my pockets. For the first time in as long as I can remember, tears start to form in my eyes, and before long they are running down my cheeks. I want to wipe them away, but I'm not going to move with the cab driver in front of me. The last thing I need is for him to look back and see me bawling coming out of a bar.

He takes me home, but I don't go inside. I don't want to go up into that empty penthouse. I want to see Charli. To hold her in my arms, to feel her soft hair beneath my chin. To get to know everything about her. We had a whirlwind relationship, and I'm not so sure I was ready to let it go. But, I tried, and she made it clear she didn't want to hear from me again.

I kick a rock out of the way as I walk along the side of the road, my mind far from where I was. The whiskey is swirling my brain, but I feel I am thinking clearly. I can't stay here and watch as the woman I love pursues her life without me. I don't know how she did it, but she won my heart over with everything she ever did. That laugh. That smile. That body. The sex.

Now that it's all gone, I see more clearly what I had—what I could have had—and I am devastated that I let it all go. I should have told her right away how I felt instead of trying to play it cool. I was too focused on playing the cool sophisticated Hollywood type, and because of that it's gone now.

I'm going to pack up my practice and move elsewhere. Somewhere the stars aren't beating down my door for a chance to go under my knife.

Somewhere I don't have to see Charli any longer. I am going to do my absolute best to forget what we could have had.

CHAPTER 12

Charli

"I'm sorry to hear that. Yeah, we've had some good times. No, no I think you should. Alright then, take care." I hear my uncle on the phone, and though he is still his cold, distant self, he does seem a little disappointed.

"Did you lose an actor?" I ask, but he barely glances my way.

"Nah, Dr. Carr is leaving," he replies nonchalantly. I feel a twinge in my heart.

"Leaving? Where is he going?" I try to sound disinterested, but I can sense that it's not working. My uncle, however, is too wrapped up in himself to notice anything that I'm doing.

"I think he said New York. I don't know, don't care really. Why do you?"

"I don't."

I say that, but I know I do care. I care a lot. What I don't know, is why. Throughout the day, it just eats away at me that he is leaving, and I know I should go see him. Perhaps it's the guilt. Although I'm still hurt and rather angry, I never felt good about not giving him the chance to explain himself. He was very kind to me, and I should have at least given him that.

After arguing with myself most of the morning, I decide I'm going to go see him after I'm done at the studio.

I STEP out of the cab with my heart pounding. The entire ride I worried about how Dirk would react to seeing me again—would he be angry? That's what I expect.

But the opposite happens. When he opens his door and looks at me, I can see that he is surprised and thrilled. But, the sight of him makes me angry.

"How dare you?" In my head, I'm screaming. I'm glad that my voice comes out in a low, reasonably normal tone. He looks at me with a solemn expression.

"Charli, I am so sorry—but that was a misunderstanding. She was an old fling who showed up here uninvited, I—"

"You just had her in for what? A talk?" I'm fuming. I thought I was going to come here to have a reasonable conversation, but I didn't realize just how much anger I was hanging onto.

"No! She pushed her way in, and I didn't want to be rude." He holds up his hands as he speaks. In response, I push my way past him and into his apartment.

"I thought we had something. I know that we weren't really together, yet the day after we're together I find you with another girl!" I can feel the lump in my throat, but I don't want to cry. "You ruined something that could've been great!"

"Oh, I ruined everything? Like you're going to ruin your perfect body with a surgery you don't need?" He snaps at me and I open my eyes wide. Even now he calls me perfect.

"Perfect? Perfect? You call this perfect?" I yank open my blouse, revealing my body. He takes a step forward, his hot breath heating me to my core.

"Yes, perfect," he breathes. I open my mouth, but he cuts off my words with his tongue, thrusting himself down my throat. Though I am taken by surprise, I am ready. I'm angry and filled with lust, and all I want is to prove to him how perfect I can be. He grabs my bra and tears it open from the front, and I do the same to his shirt.

I roll the garment off his shoulders, and he lifts me onto the counter. His hands are on the buckle of my pants, and my hands are on his jeans. We are still fiercely kissing each other. I bite his shoulder.

He cries out, and I can see that I have aroused him even further. He lifts me from the counter and carries me to the bedroom, all the while I am running my hands down his strong back.

He falls over me on the bed, using his hand to stop himself as his mouth comes down to meet mine once more. His hands are on my bare breasts, then his mouth. His teeth bite my nipple and I moan.

I try to go down on him, but he holds my hands above my head and begins biting and kissing me, moving all the way down to my panties. He uses his teeth to remove them, and his hot breath makes me even wetter. I moan as he glides his tongue between my lips. I grab his head with my hands, running my fingers through his hair. In an instant, he is back at my face, kissing me with more passion than I have ever felt.

"I need you," I whisper. "I need you inside me."

He smiles as he reaches down, and I brace myself. I love how rough he is—like he can't hold himself back. I love that moment when he enters me, and I feel him filling me up to the brink of orgasm with just one thrust. He eases himself partially inside me before thrusting himself hard.

I cry out sensually and run my nails down his back, hard. I can feel that I have dug deep, but the moans and cries he makes tell me that he is enjoying himself as much as I am. I roll over him and get on top, riding him hard. All the while his hands are on my breasts, and then his tongue follows his hands. We fight for who gets to be on top, and once again, I find myself writhing beneath him.

We are both close, and our breathing deepens as we near climax. Before, I would have closed my eyes and let the moment wash over me, but now, I lock eyes with him. I can see the passion in his face, then I feel him twitch inside me right as I feel myself explode with pleasure. I can hardly breathe as I am consumed with complete bliss.

He continues to gently move back and forth inside me for a heavenly minute, then he rolls off and I lay my head on his chest.

We lay in silence for a couple minutes as we both catch our breath.

"Are you really leaving?" I ask, looking up at him. He nods.

"I don't think LA has much to offer me anymore."

"Where will you go?"

"New York. Chicago. I don't know. Women want to be fixed all over the place."

I lay silently for a while, thinking. There is so much I want to say, but nothing seems to take form in my mind.

"I'm not going to go through with it," I say quietly.

"Through with what?"

"The surgery. You've convinced me. If my uncle has a problem with it, he can sue me." I give him a playfully defiant look, and he laughs.

"Well, I've got a lawyer if he does," Dirk says. He then adds, "Why don't you come with me?"

I look at him in surprise.

"I'm serious. Come with me. We can make this work, I know we can. You have what it takes to be an actress, you just need to be out of this environment. Come on, Charli, you know you want to." He kisses my forehead and I lean back.

As much as I hate to admit it, he's right. This lifestyle I thought was everything I wanted isn't for me. I want to get away from here and start life fresh somewhere else—with him.

I want to leave all this behind—my uncle, the set, everything. It's a gamble, and a gamble isn't something that I often take, but I want to.

I want to give us a try.

After a moment, I nod. "Alright, Dr. Carr, you've convinced me."

He looks at me for a moment, not entirely sure if I am serious.

"I'll go with you."

He looks amazed. "Are you sure?"

"Yes," I say. And I am. I've never been more sure of anything in my life.

The End.

SIGN UP TO RECEIVE FREE BOOKS

Sign Up to Receive Free E-Books and Audiobook Codes.

Would you like to read **The Unexpected Nanny, Dirty Little Virgin** and **other romance books** for **free?**

You can sign up to receive these free e-books and audiobooks by typing this link into your browser:

https://www.steamyromance.info/free-books-and-audiobooks-hot-and-steamy/

Or this one:

https://www.steamyromance.info/the-unexpected-nanny-free/

PREVIEW OF WHIPS AND CHAINS
A BILLIONAIRE & A VIRGIN ROMANCE

By Celeste Fall

Synopsis

As a teenager, growing up dirt-poor, beautiful, brainy Tracie Rutherford knew education was her ticket out of this Skunk's Hollow cycle of poverty. Consequently, she developed a reputation as an "ice maiden." But her hard work paid off in the shape of a full scholarship to the University of Georgia. Meeting handsome, charismatic billionaire Jamie Spelling seemed like a dream come true. Still a virgin, Tracie's first sexual experience with her seasoned lover was mind-blowing. Jamie's mother's disapproval of this "trollop" who had forced her way into their family was palpable. She was simply "not their kind." But Tracie's honest, eager attitude won the hearts of Jamie's grandmother, Audra Spelling, and her companion, bold, brassy billionaire rancher, Lottie Chambers. When Jamie's sexual fantasies and his demands made Tracie realize she was merely a commodity to please her husband's rich clients, she sought the help of these two women who helped her realize her potential.

When University of Georgia freshman Jamie Spellman spies strikingly beautiful economics classmate Tracie Rutherford, it was lust at first sight. Unaccustomed to being denied anything—or anyone—he wants, Jamie is shocked and fascinated to discover the beautiful, blonde, brainy girl is still a virgin. A whirlwind romance culminates in Jamie's taking Tracie for his bride. His billionaire parents are unimpressed as his mother has already selected a wealthy girl with the proper pedigree for her only son. Follow the downward spiral of this increasingly depraved relationship to discover if love conquers all.

"I will not spend my life in poverty and pregnancy in Skunk's Hollow!" teenage Tracie Rutherford promises herself. She dreams of a life where money and success are possible. When she meets darkly handsome billionaire Jamie Spellman, it seems like her fairy-tale dream is at last coming true. Still a virgin, the brainy economics student is swept off her feet by Jamie's wining and dining and sexual antics. Little does Tracie know the price she will pay for success. Follow Tracie's adventure as her life takes strange turns

CHAPTER ONE

Not in My Backyard

Thirty-one-year-old Tracie Spellman pushed her artfully streaked blonde hair out of her eyes and reached blindly for the Snooze button on her annoyingly persistent alarm clock. Her head throbbed. Her body ached. It even hurt to open and close her eyes.

With a groan, she rolled over. That's when she noticed the blood-streaked sheets and the stickiness between her legs.

What the hell happened last night?

While she was trying to collect her senses and her recollections, a sharp knock sounded at the door. Tracie squinted at the clock. Her head pounded.

8:04

Christ! Who'd be bothering her at this hour?

The door opened and in whisked her secretary, Avril Steele. Her Prada shoes clicked purposefully on the shiny oak floor as she bustled briskly across the spacious room to Tracie's bedside.

She fixed her steely gray eyes on Tracie's disheveled appearance and sniffed in distain. Tracie was pretty sure her prim British assistant could smell sex in the air around her.

"What do you want, Avril?" Tracie groaned. She knew her assistant's presence at this hour couldn't be a good sign.

"Madame," Avril began, glancing pointedly at her watch, "when Master Jamie left for work over an hour ago, he asked me to wake you and remind you of your meeting with Mrs. Chambers at nine."

"Oh, no! Is that today?" The pounding in her head increased to jackhammer intensity.

"Well, this is July 8, so, yes, the meeting is today," Avril replied patiently, as if she were talking to a three-year-old.

Tracie hated Avril's condescending attitude. The efficient, yet irritating, forty-year-old had not been Tracie's choice. She hadn't wanted an assistant at all. But if she was forced to hire one, she wanted someone who was younger and more fun. But Jamie, as always, had the last word. He insisted that his attractive wife needed someone who would "keep her on track" and "establish a routine" in Tracie's life. In other words, someone to whom Tracie would be accountable when Jamie was at work.

When Tracie and Jamie had met at college and fallen in love, the poor girl from the wrong side of the tracks in her small southern Alabama town of Skunk's Hollow had had no idea how wide a gap separated their lives.

Tracie was in for her first rude awakening when Jamie brought her home to his massive Montgomery estate. Her mind traveled back while Avril strode to her closet to select an appropriate outfit for her meeting.

With a quiet groan, Tracie gathered the soiled sheets around her and headed for the shower. She had no energy for sparring with meddlesome Lottie Chambers today.

Why does Jamie get her involved in these touchy issues? she wondered. *Or, is this the work of his mother?*

When she'd met the intimidating Marilyn Spellman, it had been hate at first sight. The dark-haired, statuesque matriarch had left nothing to the imagination. She loathed Tracie's mere existence.

And as for this little gold digger ever being part of my family? Never! Charity might begin at home, but not in my son's bedroom! according to Marilyn.

All efforts on Jamie's part to negotiate a truce between the two women he loved most fell on unresponsive ears. Marilyn Spellman might be the undisputed champion of fundraisers for local food banks and homeless shelters. But when it came to her family? She didn't care a fig about how Tracie had pulled herself out of the slums and graduated top of her class at Emory. She would never be welcome under Marilyn's roof. All Jamie's eloquent pleading to his mother to put herself in Tracie's shoes had no effect on Marilyn. Her mind was made up. This girl was bad news, and the sooner Jamie came to his senses and dumped her, the better!

To be fair, Tracie admitted, she and Jamie's mother did not get off on the right foot when Marilyn burst into Jamie's bedroom and found Tracie on her knees in front of Jamie, performing fellatio. Two nights in widely separated bedrooms had taken their toll on the pair accustomed to sleeping together at Emory. They were merely getting reacquainted and letting off some pent-up sexual steam.

Marilyn didn't see it that way. She was convinced Tracie was a low-life, promiscuous woman who would fall upon whatever was put in front of her. The Spellman wealth was not going to become this girl's opportunity, if Marilyn had anything to say about it. She had pretty socialite Tiffany King in her sights, as soon as she could make her son see things sensibly. Tiffany would be a fine match. She was their kind of people!

So the two women gave each other a wide berth. Jamie never took Tracie home again, until she was wearing his grandmother's diamond engagement ring. There was nothing Marilyn Spellman could do except pitch a fit. The three-carat diamond belonged to Jamie's paternal grandmother, Audra Spellman, who adored Tracie and was thrilled to pass on the family heirloom to her only grandson and his bride-to-be. Marilyn did a slow burn and waited for the right moment to rid the family of this white trash.

Audra also insisted upon hosting and paying for the wedding. Tracie was torn. She hadn't been home or talked to her parents since she graduated from high school. She wanted them to know she was doing well, but she didn't want to rub their noses in her success. Although they could make the trip to Audra's mansion in Montgomery, it was unlikely that they'd even consider it. They wouldn't know how to dress, how to act, or how to talk to these people. Meeting her parents would give Marilyn Spellman further fuel to highlight the gap between Jamie and Tracie. The Spellmans and the Rutherfords were as different as two sides of a coin, as sharply contrasting as black and white, as likely to hit it off as fire and gas. It was a disaster waiting to happen! Tracie had worked so hard to rid herself of the stench of Skunk's Hollow. She was reluctant to bring the two disparate sides of her life together. She'd moved on and worked hard to make a new life for herself.

CHAPTER TWO

Avril's Dilemma

As she gathered the ripped, soiled sheet around her and headed to the bathroom, Tracie could hear Avril's muttering in the cavernous walk-in closet where she was selecting the "least inappropriate" outfit for Tracie to wear to this important meeting with Lottie Chambers. She paused for a moment, wondering if she should shoo Avril out of her closet. Then, with a shrug and an evil little smile, she continued on her way to the bathroom. "Let the old bat think whatever she wants," Tracie muttered.

AVRIL SAW her job as a daily battle of wills to try to mold the reluctant Tracie into the family representative. Marilyn and Alan Spellman would have wanted for their son and her to be part of Spellman Investments. She'd been at it ever since Tracie had become Jamie's bride at age twenty-eight. But, so far, it was a losing battle. The Spellmans had offered Avril handsome financial incentives for whipping their daughter-in-law into shape. In a battle of wills, Avril was usually up for the challenge. But, it seemed that she'd met her match. Tracie wasn't like the other pampered, spoiled little rich girls whom Avril had been sent to dispatch after Master Jamie had awakened to find the inconvenient conquest resting her head on his shoulder. Tracie was a tough nut with street smarts. Clearly, she had no notion of being spirited away by the intimidating Avril. This girl had substance. Avril was grudgingly appreciative of her backbone—if not her manners or her deplorable taste in clothing.

TRUE, the Spellmans had won a battle when Avril was chosen as the new Mrs. Spellman's secretary. There was no doubt that she'd never have been Tracie's choice. Avril knew she wasn't young enough or hip enough or fun enough to suit Tracie. The young blonde acted like a teenager. She had no idea what her role should be—nor did she seem to care. And as for Master Jamie? He was so smitten—fuckstruck, Avril thought to herself—that he couldn't see how his wife's attitude was hurting his reputation and that of the company. Spellman Financial could not afford a false step. Avril had heard Jamie and his father discussing some bad investments and their need to woo new clients and offer incentives to their present clients to stay. She knew that, if the company hoped to stay afloat, the Spellmans had to do some fancy manipulating. Frankly, Avril did not see the new Mrs. Spellman as an asset in that department.

HOWEVER, Avril knew how important it was for Tracie to make a good impression on Lottie Chambers. Tracie seemed unaware or unconcerned about how much was riding on this meeting. Avril shook her head in dismay as she scrutinized Tracie's wardrobe. Nothing here spoke of business and good breeding. At best, the clothes were frivolous. And at worst, they were simply poorly designed and bad fashion sense.

As she worked her way down the rows of clothing arranged in no particular order, Avril made a note to return to the closet and establish some order with the maid who picked up after Tracie dropped her clothes anywhere. She had just about come to the end of the massive closet when her hand hit a leather garment in the dark corner. When she pulled it off the rod, she gasped in horror. Hanging from a padded hanger was a black leather bustier. In a box below it, she discovered thigh-high black leather boots and a whip with braided lashes that ended in metal studs. What appeared to be blood coated several of the studs.

Avril pulled back her hand as if she'd been burned. *What on earth is this girl playing at?*

Unable to resist, Avril plunged her hand farther into the box. The next item she pulled out was a set of fur-lined handcuffs. There were a handful of silk scarves in various stages of wrinkle and knot. Out came a giant purple feather. Then, in the very bottom of the box, Avril extracted a pair of shiny black leather gloves. Examining them closely, she noted a greasy substance, which looked suspiciously like Vaseline, coated the palms and fingers. Avril shuddered and swallowed deep breaths to keep from being sick.

. . .

What on earth were these two up to? she wondered. She recalled the blood-stained sheet, which appeared to have slits cut into its Egyptian cotton threads. Images rose unbidden to her troubled mind.

Should I report this to the Spellmans? Should I mention it to Master Jamie? Was he part of this, or were the things I found part of Tracie's sordid past?

AVRIL DECIDED to do nothing until she knew more about what was going on. This might have been a costume for a masquerade. Rich people had strange diversions. She quickly snapped photos of the garments and the other paraphernalia with her phone.

THEN, with a sigh, she chose the least objectionable of Tracie's outfits and left it on a chair by the bathroom door.

CHAPTER THREE

Like a Virgin

Hot water flowed over Tracie's aching body. With a soft washcloth, she probed the depths of her core, wincing as her sweet spot proved to be anything else but sweet. As she lathered her body and hair with the rich lavender products she liked, she tried to recreate the events of the night before.

SHE RECALLED a loud party and far too much champagne. She remembered someone—it might have been Jamie—feeding her toast points piled high with beluga caviar. She knew she'd washed it down with the finest vodka money could buy.

SHE HAD no idea how she'd gotten to bed or who had undressed her.

* * *

WHERE ARE MY CLOTHES? Did I hang them up?

SHE HAD a foggy idea of whips and chains and four-inch high heels on hip-high boots with spurs.

DID I DREAM ALL THIS? If so, why are the sheets blood smeared? Had the sex been that rough? She didn't think so. Sure, she was sore. But there were no lacerations.

THEN, who bled on the sheets?

WITH A CONTENTED SMILE, Tracie recalled her first meeting with Jamie. She was majoring in political science, and Jamie was getting a business degree. Their programs both required introductory economics and statistics. Tracie noticed the handsome, auburn-haired hunk with the surfer's body. He'd glanced at her, his startling green eyes sweeping over her. After their first economics seminar, he'd introduced himself and invited her for coffee. They'd talked about everything: new movies, music they enjoyed, books they'd read. They laughed over classmates' bizarre behavior. Jamie had her in stitches when he mimicked their professors.

When Jamie walked her back to her dorm, he'd leaned in and placed a butterfly-light kiss on her forehead. "See you tomorrow, Tracie Rutherford," he'd called back over his shoulder.

* * *

THE NEXT DAY, he'd called to ask her to work on a statistics assignment together. Tracie was so smitten with the gorgeous, popular boy with the killer smile that she could scarcely wait to get to class each day.

THERE FOLLOWED A WHIRLWIND ROMANCE. In the city no longer than she had been, Jamie seemed to know the *in* places. They ate in some amazing Atlanta restaurants, attended sporting events, concerts, and theater.

THEY WENT for long drives in the BMW coup his parents had given him for graduation and engaged in some heavy petting that steamed up the windows of the baby blue automobile. "Your first time is going to be memorable," Jamie told her one night when they both withdrew, panting with longing.

"How—how did you know I'm a virgin?" she asked. "Oh, no! I'm a complete novice, aren't I?"

"NO!" Jamie assured her. "You give head very enthusiastically."

"THEN I KISS LIKE A SIX-YEAR-OLD!" Tracie wailed.

"OF COURSE NOT!" Jamie assured her, planting kisses on her nose, her chin, and her forehead. "Your kisses send me to take cold showers."

"THEN WHAT GAVE ME AWAY?" she asked sadly.

. . .

"Promise you won't get mad?" Jamie demanded.

"Just tell me," Tracie snapped.

"Well," Jamie continued, "I've never met a girl who creamed her pants just sitting beside me. It's very flattering. I promise, your first time will be mind-blowing."

Jamie had been as good as his word. They'd dined at an expensive Atlanta steakhouse complete with flowers at the table, a violinist to serenade them, and champagne.

The champagne had made Tracie sneeze. She was giddy after the second glass.

Then they'd walked up the street, arms around one another, to a posh hotel where Jamie had reserved the bridal suite. They'd feasted on chocolate-covered strawberries and more champagne as they soaked in the heart-shaped hot tub. Then, they'd taken a shower in the enormous walk-in shower stall, where they'd lathered each other with eucalyptus shower gel. Jamie explored every crevice of her body and dried every inch of her throbbing body with a fluffy white towel.

Then, in spite of her pleading, Jamie had patiently and thoroughly caressed, kissed, and suckled every part of her body. When she was a squealing mass of hormones, Jamie began what could only be called cock teasing, inserting his throbbing member into Tracie an inch and then pulling out. This went on for what seemed like hours as Tracie clutched and raked his back and thrust herself at him. The final thrust was such a relief that Tracie scarcely noticed the pain or the bleeding.

THEIR LOVEMAKING EXTENDED WELL into the night. Tracie just couldn't get enough of this heady new experience, and Jamie, in his sexual prime, was literally up for the task.

AFTERWARD, Jamie gently sponged her throbbing crotch and covered her with a sheet. He planted gentle kisses on her face and whispered, "Good night, princess."

WHEN TRACIE AWOKE the next morning, Jamie had breakfast waiting. She quickly brushed her teeth, took a quick shower, and surveyed herself in the mirror. Her skin glowed and she could not wipe the smile off her face.

WRAPPED in fluffy white hotel robes, the two ate a hearty breakfast. Then Jamie asked her what she wanted to do with the day.

"DON'T YOU HAVE A CLASS?" Tracie asked him.

"I AM OFFICIALLY AT YOUR DISPOSAL," Jamie answered.

. . .

"Then I know exactly how I want to spend my day," Tracie announced. "What time do we have to be out of here?"

"Not for hours," Jamie replied. "I just put the Do Not Disturb sign on the door."

"Then, you can proceed any time," Tracie said.

"You're lucky I am at my sexual prime and can meet your needs," Jamie pointed out.

"Yes, I am," Tracie agreed, reaching for him.

CHAPTER FOUR

Whatever It Takes

When people talked about being "swept off their feet" and "love at first sight," practical Tracie Rutherford scoffed outright. For her, there was no poetry and candlelight and violin music. She'd devoted her entire miserable life to escaping the abject poverty of her situation.

Her life had been one struggle after another. The fifth child of seven, she saw what it meant to wear hand-me-downs that had been patched over patches. She knew what it felt like to endure hunger pangs because fried bread was all that was available for breakfast, and her lunch consisted of apples from the tree behind their three-bedroom cabin and leftover breakfast bread—if such a thing existed. Her parents worked from dawn to dusk to scrabble crops from the poor, sandy soil that surrounded their house. By the time they paid the rent on the property, there was precious little to buy flour, sugar, and seeds for the next crop.

As a child, Tracie didn't feel resentful. None of the other kids in the one-room school the Rutherford kids attended had anything either. But Tracie had one thing the others did not have: The strikingly beautiful little girl had a burning desire to escape the poverty in which she'd grown up. As she watched her older sisters and brothers marry and sink into the same hopeless existence her parents lived, she vowed that she'd make something of herself. She'd get out of Skunk's Hollow and never look back.

Besides being beautiful, Tracie Rutherford had smarts. She was book smart and she was street smart. She avoided the boys of Skunk's Hollow and the surrounding communities like the plague. Though they sniffed around her like dogs in heat, Tracie was not about to jeopardize her escape plan by lying with any of them. Sex with those boys could end in only one thing: a life of hard work, starvation, and popping out a kid every year until mercifully, menopause took care of that or her reproductive system just collapsed. She'd seen what happened to her mother and the other neighbor ladies: dull-eyed, toothless creatures who looked twenty years older than their actual age. Tracie was not about to fall into that trap.

So Tracie developed a reputation for being uppity, a cock tease, someone who thought she was better than everybody else. This only intensified the male interest in getting into her pants. Tracie's high school years at nearby Alabaster High were marked by scuffles in the stairwells, where her classmates tried to grope her, and skirmishes behind closed classroom doors, where the randy PE teacher attempted to cop a feel under the guise of helping her explore her sexuality.

Exhausted by fending off these unwanted advances, Tracie sought the help of her guidance counselor, a world-weary sixty-year-old named Amanda Aimes. Her meeting with Miss Aimes was the luckiest thing that happened to the sixteen-year-old. It was no accident that the red-haired, green-eyed woman had chosen guidance. Herself a product of the dirt-farm existence in lower Alabama, Amanda Aimes had used her academic ability to escape the cycle of misery she saw in her community. Having endured the snide comments, sexual assaults, and physical abuse of her family and neighbors, Amanda had been befriended by her high school guidance teacher.

Lydia Percy took Amanda under her wing. She helped her apply for scholarships and assisted her with settling in at Emory, where she got a teaching degree. Although Amanda had vowed never to return to southern Alabama, when the guidance position came up at Alabaster, Amanda took it as a sign that she should "pay it forward." To that end, she had been helping people like Tracie escape their past for thirty years now.

When Tracie secured a full scholarship to the University of Georgia, just outside Atlanta, she was the happiest girl in the world. She loved the fact that this flagship college touting itself as the birthplace of higher education was not in a big city. She vowed she'd make Miss Aimes proud of her. With money given to her by the guidance staff, she bought a one-way bus ticket to Athens, Georgia.

Tracie—who'd hardly ever been outside Alabaster and Skunk's Hollow—fell immediately in love with this university town an hour northeast of Atlanta. With a population of over a hundred thousand, this sixth-largest Georgia city had the feel of a large town. The University of Georgia was literally a town within a town. Tracie also liked the sense of history of the campus.

Its first buildings had actually been made from logs. Lots around the campus were sold in the early 1800s to raise money to build more university buildings. When the first class graduated in 1804, the town of Athens had only three homes, three stores, and a few other buildings on Front Street. This street was later renamed Broad Street. Franklin College, completed in 1806, was the University of Georgia's first permanent structure. This brick building—named in honor of Ben Franklin—was still standing and called Old College. As she walked through the campus grounds, Tracie felt like she belonged here, that she was a part of an American heritage.

She silently blessed Miss Aimes for giving her this opportunity. And she made a pledge that she would do her best to make this precious gift pay off. Tracie studied campus maps eagerly, familiarizing herself with the bookstore, her dorm building, and the buildings where her classes would be held. She took the self-guided campus tour, made a trip to the UGA Visitors' Center, and checked the UGA Master Calendar to see what events were happening on campus each day. She was grateful that Miss Aimes had suggested she arrive a week earlier than registration so she had a feel for her surroundings before the crowds started to descend.

When the first day of classes rolled around, Tracie was armed with textbooks, a tablet, and UGA sweatshirts. As she headed across campus with her UGA backpack slung over her shoulder, she felt like a college student.

"Let the adventure begin," she cried, throwing her arms into the sultry, southern, subtropical air.

She had no idea what adventures awaited her.

**If you want to continue reading this story,
you can get your copy from your favorite
vendor by searching for the title:**

Whips and Chains

A Billionaire & A Virgin Romance

You can also find the e-book version by typing this link in your computer's browser:

https://www.hotandsteamyromance.com/products/whips-and-chains-a-billionaire-a-virgin-romance

OTHER BOOKS BY THIS AUTHOR

Saving Her Rescuer: A Billionaire & A Virgin Romance

I was just trying to get away from my crazy ex for the weekend when I ended up in a giant pileup on the highway up to Gore Mountain.

https://geni.us/SavingHerRescuer

~

Sensual Sounds: A Rockstar Ménage

Lust. Lies. Double lives.

The rock and roll industry is full of people who are looking out for themselves and willing to do anything to rise to the top.

https://www.hotandsteamyromance.com/collections/frontpage/products/sensual-sounds-a-rockstar-menage

~

On the Run: A Secret Baby Romance

Murder. Lies. Fraud. Just another day in the lives of billionaires and women on the run.

https://www.hotandsteamyromance.com/collections/frontpage/products/on-the-run-a-secret-baby-romance

~

The Dirty Doctor's Touch: A Billionaire Doctor Romance

I am a master. An elitist. I am at the top of my field, and I know what I am doing.

https://www.hotandsteamyromance.com/collections/frontpage/products/the-dirty-doctor-s-touch-a-billionaire-doctor-romance

The Hero She Needs: A Single Daddy Next Door Romance

He's the only man I've ever wanted...

https://www.hotandsteamyromance.com/collections/frontpage/products/the-hero-she-needs-a-single-daddy-next-door-romance

You can find all of my books here:

Hot and Steamy Romance

https://www.hotandsteamyromance.com

Facebook

facebook.com/HotAndSteamyRomance

COPYRIGHT

©Copyrights 2020 by Alizeh Valentine- All rights Reserved
In no way is it legal to reproduce, duplicate, or transmit any part of this document in either electronic means or in printed format. Recording of this publication is strictly prohibited and any storage of this document is not allowed unless with written permission from the publisher. All rights are reserved.
Respective authors own all copyrights not held by the publisher.

www.ingramcontent.com/pod-product-compliance
Lightning Source LLC
LaVergne TN
LVHW011732060526
838200LV00051B/3159